Cherry Smyth is an Irish writer, living in London. Her first two poetry collections, *When the Lights Go Up*, 2001 and *One Wanted Thing*, 2006 were published by Lagan Press. Her third collection, *Test, Orange*, 2012, and fourth, *Famished*, 2019 were published by Pindrop Press. Her debut novel, *Hold Still*, Holland Park Press, appeared in 2013. *Famished* tours as a performance in collaboration with vocalist Lauren Kinsella and composer Ed Bennett. Cherry was nominated as a Fellow for the Royal Society of Literature in 2022 and is also a Hawthornden Fellow. She is Associate Professor in Creative & Critical Writing at the University of Greenwich.

Craig Jordan-Baker has published fiction in New Writing, Text, Firefly Magazine, Potluck and the époque press é-zine. His drama has been widely performed in the UK and he has had work commissioned by institutions such as The National Archives, Brighton Museums and the Theatre Royal Brighton. Craig lives in Brighton and is a Senior Lecturer in Creative Writing at the University of Brighton. *The Nacullians,* Craig's debut novel, was published by époque press in 2020.

If the River is Hidden has also been developed as a performance piece with the flautist Eimear McGeown.

If the River is Hidden

Cherry Smyth &
Craig Jordan-Baker

époque press

Published by époque press in 2022
www.epoquepress.com

Typeset in Usual Light/Light Italic/Regular
& Aupress Regular.
Typsetting & cover design by **Ten Storeys®**

Printed in the United Kingdom by Clays Ltd,
Elcograf S.p.A.

British Library Cataloguing-in-Publication Data
A catalogue record for this book is available from
the British Library

ISBN 978-1-7391881-0-8 (Paperback edition)

To fresh water

Scan here to access a unique composition by flautist Eimear McGeown, specially commissioned to accompany this book. Through traditional tunes, blues, disco and improvisations using tin whistle, classical and traditional flute, Eimear's musical collage evokes the textures, rhythms and depths of our journey along the River Bann.

'Whatever stains you, you rubbed it into yourselves,'
Seamus Heaney

Now there is only the river
that was always on its own way,'
W.S. Merwin

'Because even a river can be lonely,
even a river will die of thirst.'
Natalie Diaz

Preface

She is driving south down the A26, from Portstewart. She is on her way, eventually, to West Cork. It will be late when she gets there, and perhaps she imagines the flicker of fire through an old window, the gasp and boom of the Atlantic behind it. But she's got a long way to go yet. The little car creeps west, south, west, as it works an awkward arc around Lough Neagh, Ireland's eye.

The roads are quieter than before the pandemic and a scattering of car, truck, car scumbles on towards Belfast. She thinks again of her destination, of the end of the journey, but then, a sign approaches her, a sign for the town of Banbridge, Co. Down. The sign passes soon enough, but she begins to think. She remembers that Banbridge is where his grandfather was from, was where he visited as a child, where he got drunk and giddy on the banks of the Bann, where they teased him about his English accent and where he saw Union Jacks everywhere and thought, 'Aren't they trying just a bit too hard to be British?'

Yes, the river Bann, Northern Ireland's longest, its source not so far from Banbridge, in the Mourne Mountains. She

1

knows she has to find it and that he would be the one to help her. And then she thinks of the Barmouth, Portstewart, where the Bann meets the ocean. Of growing up near the slow, wide swathe of the river which began as a trickle. She grew up looking at the sea, not the river which wound seaward behind the sandhills, out of sight. She did not miss the river like she missed the waves. She did not know the riverbank like she knew the strand, where she had sat and watched the small pilot boats meet tankers in the bay to guide them into the Barmouth and up between the hidden sandbanks to the inland harbour at Coleraine.

She had spent four months of lockdown in West Cork and she realises that it's the longest time she's been in Ireland since she left after university, like so many others, in the 1980s. It has wobbled her stance, unsettled her core. The stance of having left, the core of never coming back. She has walked the Caha Mountains but not the Mournes. She has fished the Kenmare River but not the Bann. Some part of her wants to learn the North again, learn the river, walk home along it. Some part won't let go. It's a path leading north, a body of water that knows where to go. It's some part that is family, that is longing, some part that wants to be near her old home, her old Dad, to help care for him. Some part that doesn't want to get that phone call in London. She feels this instinct like the river feels its course. For a while, she forgets about her destination out west, is happy just to travel. The idea of the river Goddess, *an Bhanna*, is on her.

A couple of days later and she's calling him in Brighton. How's the Beara? How're your folks? He's glad to talk to her but there's something washed-out in his voice, a heavy teaching load and the leadenness of Covid-time. She starts to tell him about the long drive out west and the sign for Banbridge.

How it rushed upon her and just as quicky passed away. How it left an image of the river. The Bann should be walked, she says, and he should walk it with her.

'Of course!' he spurts, but then is coy: keen not to seem too keen. The idea of an adventure when he's spent the last year on his arse in his small flat, the last year standing up in his small flat, the last year sweating and shivering and stalling in his fucking small flat.

'Well yes', he says, as moderately as he can, 'I will, yes.' But he thinks to himself, why would we walk the Bann, why follow the river?

*

His first choice is the tome of an atlas, open on the floor. But soon, he's zooming in and out of online maps, caught in the spate of a static kind of travel. He traces the river with eye, finger, mouse-pointer and realises as he does, that rivers are already stories. They have beginnings, middles, endings, and make the most satisfying of lines. He knows though, that story and reality are not, or not always, the same thing. Some stories are too simple to believe in, too straight, too easy to trace. But the reality of the river may tell a new story, he thinks.

And as he traces the line of the Bann from south to north of the statelet that is Northern Ireland, he notes too that map and reality are not, or not always, the same thing. Since it was carved out from six of Ulster's nine counties, its borders, its names, its people and its history have resisted the too-easy lines on maps, the too-simple stories. The course of this place seems to be drifting, slowly. Will this be celebrated, marked, protested, ignored? Will lines solidify, or dance and fizzle even more? The river may show us, he thinks.

His mind buzzes with the potential as he glides the cursor's compass over the screen. They will take a journey to the place he has always dreamed toward, though never lived in. Banbridge, the North, Ireland. It's some part that is family, that is longing. There is some part of him that wants to be near an old home. There is some part of him that doesn't want to keep to maps. The idea of the river Goddess is upon him too.

Days pass, OS maps are bought and the Bann is marked as it passes through Sheet 29 (the Mournes), Sheet 8 (Ballymoney) and Sheet 19 (Armagh). Crudely, he rulers-out the miles on the sheets for the whole journey. 84 miles, give or take. He tells her he wants to stick to using physical maps, to enjoy the working out of the path and the working round of the river. To embrace the uncertainty inherent in not having your position geolocated by dozens of satellites in near-earth orbit. Uncertainty, it seems to them both, is key. For why go on a journey of discovery if you both know exactly where you are, know exactly which degrees of longitude and latitude will constitute where you end up?

When he was thirteen, he got his first tattoo. Curlicues of black ink were filled in with emerald-isle green, in a fag-fugged studio in the backend of Southampton city centre in 1996. With a fresh shamrock on his barely-teenage arm, he announced his intention to be involved in all things Irish, as well as his intention to avoid all teachers when changing for PE.

The feat bemused and impressed his peers in equal measure. Of course, tattoos were edgy, and being the first boy to do one of those *first-things* that edgy boys do, marked him out. There on his arm were the beginnings of a transformation and a rejection of the English boy he was. Already, he had plied his grandfather for stories of the North, of being a Catholic in a Protestant town, of emigration, of being an outsider in a new country. He had savoured and lived the tales, but knew the tales didn't belong solely to him, and so he had sought out ink to colour his own mind. How, his friends asked, could a grandfather from the arse end of potatoland inspire such a sigil of devotion? Why would anyone want to be a thick fucking paddy, with their little people, their twiddle-de-de and their machine guns? Why read O'Casey, Wilde, Heaney, Joyce, when half of it doesn't even make sense? Though, for this English boy, it made better sense than England.

He understood later that it was all about class. Or maybe class and geography. The cliché goes that geography is destiny, but when you're a working-class kid from the arse end of a Southampton council estate, no one uses the word *destiny*. It's not even called *fate*. It's just called *life*, and any other words for it will mark you out as pompous. But maybe he wanted to be a little pompous, maybe he didn't want to belong to the life of his arse-end estate.

So, he involved himself in the life of that place, that nation, two nations, that were not, he was assured, really his. Like many others, he picked a side in the Troubles, based on little more than a grandfather's stories. But every sip he took of that place, he found nothing wanting. When he wanted simplicity, there was a land of frugal comfort and the certainty of an island's shape. When he wanted fantasy, Queen Medb and Cú Chulainn would warp-spasm him away from concrete and dogshit. When he wanted complexity, reading *The Plough and the Stars* and the history around it sharpened him, broadened him. Even before he had visited Ireland, he thought he better belonged there than on the estate, with its little England and its twiddle-your-fingers and its machine life. Today, he is more circumspect: keen not to seem too keen. This, of course, is difficult for a keen man, a man who is always saying yes, he will, yes.

When he tries to find a source for this journey along the Bann, then it is surely somewhere here. Of course, it really wasn't all that simple, because nothing really is, but he's a writer now, and writers have that job of putting small dams into life and seeing what wells there.

*

When she was sixteen, she was dressed for badminton in the Church Hall, but aiming for Spuds, the local disco, with a ribbed polo in her bag. Green eyeshadow and lippy she'd apply in the public loo off the Diamond, in the pocket of her flares. Of course they all thought about bombs – this was a pub in the North in 1976 – but any fear yielded to a fierce sense of adolescent destiny: if you were meant to die, so be it. No one liked to mention being left maimed. She'd grown up on the north coast of the North, looking north and seeing the South, County Donegal, part of the Republic, the Free State, as her grandfather called it, in a tone in which free sounded like fake or foul. She'd known seven years of 'The Troubles' and vowed to leave the North as soon as she left school. She'd go south and claim a less troubled Irishness, an Irishness bolstered by writers, an identity you could read yourself into.

So, she book-wormed her way through James Joyce, Elizabeth Bowen, Frank O'Connor, Mary Lavin, Seamus Heaney, William Trevor and others, letting complexities of class and geography ride out on the beauty and awe of a metaphor. She would go to Trinity, in the steps of many middle-class Protestants, like Oscar Wilde and Samuel Beckett before her: she didn't know then that Catholics were only admitted in 1793, and that the Catholic Church later banned Catholics from studying there from 1871-1970. She didn't know that in choosing Trinity she was treading in a lineage of Protestant control and discrimination, the very reason for the Troubles in the first place.

The summer before she left for college, for a cramped flat share in Rathmines, is both indistinct and keenly luminous. She was eighteen and a disco freak. She bumped to the beat of Chic, KC & The Sunshine Band and Boney M. She fell asleep to the charts on Radio Luxembourg playing on a white trannie. She never listened to the news. She worked part time in her dad's shop. She shared a small office with another girl working a cash system called the Lamson tube, where each shop assistant sent the docket and cash in a cannister rocketing up through pneumatic tubes to a central office, where the change was counted and the cannister sucked back into the mouth of the pipe. She was touching money and taking it home. She liked its smell. Her dad had grown up in a flat above the shop. This was one of its rooms. She was in the engine of business and the belly of family. The staff had names like Meldrum and McCandless, O'Neill and Doherty and she didn't know how rare a mix that was. Or she did know, but wanted a world where this knowledge was redundant, so she kept it small, hidden and somehow safe.

One night in July, she was in Kelly's in Portrush, the clubbing mecca of the North, in an old hotel next to a caravan park, next to the sandhills. Her parents were in Donegal for the twelfth. (This is shorthand for the annual exodus from Northern Ireland for those who do not wish to witness the marching Orange Bands celebrating a victory of a Protestant king over a Catholic one in 1690) She had been dancing. A guy offered to buy her a drink. A sweet Martini. Or a Guinness and Tia Maria.

Or was it already a Southern Comfort and Orange?

Breaking news interrupted the programme on the TV above the bar. There had been three bombs in Coleraine. There was a request for all key-holders to please go the shops at once. Her dad's shop. Her name. Everyone turned to look. To pretend not to look. She left with the guy. He held her in his car. Desire rode out the fear and panic in a clutch, a kiss, the body telling itself that it was alive and that nothing else counted if you could feel this alive, this wanted. She cannot remember the rest of that night, when or how she got home, just the belief that if she didn't go home, it wouldn't have happened, that no one would be hurt. She can only remember it in the words of a poem she wrote maybe ten years later:

Not everything was destroyed. That was worse.
They sold the damage,

salvaging charred dresses, odd shoes,

scalded mannequins. Everything rained on...

I looked at faces differently.

Daddy was quiet for a long time.

When she left, she left for good. In London she became Irish, more Irish than she'd ever been. In New York she became European and missed borders and the sense of ancient time marked in stones. Her accent accrued a hint of Norf Landin and a tint of Brooklyn and when people asked where she was from, she laughed and said, 'How far back do you want to go?' And always, she travelled Ireland in her writing, and while family brought her back to the North, writing brought her back to borrowed places in Donegal, West Cork, in Monaghan and Connemara. Perhaps it was time to bring family and writing together; perhaps it was time to visit the source of both. Isn't a river a source and a symbol of a source, a mouth and an image of a mouth, bridged and touching both sides of what it divides? If his family were from the bridge of the river and hers from the mouth, surely something could be found together at the source. And if a source could speak, what would it say?

*

Down from London and up from Brighton, they meet off the train at Gatwick. They cheer at one another, bear-squeeze at this first of successful arrivals. How long is it since they've touched one another? How long have they skipped over one another's words on video calls? She thinks of the writing retreat where they first met: watching him arrive in a taxi, from her desk at a bay window, in a double-doored silence; seeing his fedora, his corduroy jacket, studded with badges, and his face riven with the cautious enthusiasm of the newly arrived. Around them, angle grinders grind and platforms are a flux of exposed rebar and the glabrous sheen of concrete. It's 2021 and a new normal is under construction.

Though they don't need to, out of instinct they have brought their passports. Her Irish one expired during lockdown, the backlog forcing her to get her first British one. His Irish one, he claimed after Brexit, like millions of diasporic others. They laugh at the irony of all this.

Slight queues move seamlessly. Sparse departure boards post small changes. They look around and realise they are doing something unusual now, by travelling. The timbre of travel itself has changed. They don their masks and try to breathe more shallowly.

From the air, the ground becomes smaller, flatter, broader. The crenulations of coasts and the silvered paths of rivers can be seen. The land turns greener, the fields narrower.

It was on the day after the summer solstice that they set out to walk the eighty-three miles from the source of the Bann to its mouth. This is the way that they went:

North and northeast from Deer's Meadow, the nebulous source of the river.

Through Katesbridge, a frost hollow where cool air creeps down, the coldest place in Ireland.

Through Banbridge town in the County Down, where the river snakes through Solitude Park and the bunting red, white and blue flickers true.

By Portadown, where a new emotion was found.

Up towards Bannfoot, where the river's upper course washes into Lough Neagh.

And then over Lough Neagh, where a silent landscape sits underwater.

Through Toome, where brickworks gouged clay from the Bann, and where the Tricolour flies.

And past Portglenone, where the Bann is broad and black.

Through Bendooragh, where they can remember little.

And to Portstewart, home of the mouth.

These were the places they were to pass on their way to the Atlantic. These were the names that staged their pilgrimage. These were the days that shortened their path.

Spelga Dam to Katesbridge

Deer's Meadow leapt its doe brown
hide through me in a London house;
Deer's Meadow, where the seeking
sought, where the journey opened
under any kind of sky. The name showed
a start – deer had been there and a deer hunter,
and it rolled its high grassiness in my city mind.
 It threw me, through me, where the journey opened,
the journey opened in my city,
where the seeking sought high grassiness.
And I saw Slieve Muck lift its snout
and bubble a clear marble of water
where we'd kneel and ask the White Cow, *Bó Finn*,
to bless our trek north, help us leave the mountain
when we'd rather not, like any hero on a quest,
whose horse is underfed and weapon blunt.
Names are the maps that preceded any map,
names are the caps that the land first wore.
Bó Finn, bless our horse, our pig, our path.

Can this be an Irish poem?

Maps are the mirrors where you see the frail line of your desire. An English child with an open atlas rolls his tongue around counties: Fermanagh, Antrim, Armagh, Tyrone. He tracks the thin lines of rivers and circles the undulations of lough edges.

Heraclitus said that you can never step into the same river twice. He didn't mention that some of us never get into the river in the first place. If the river stays in the atlas, it will always be an unchanging solid blue line, a river stepped into only once. Because most of us, most of the time, just stay at home, wherever that may be.

But the embarrassment of the map is too much for me now. The map is too thin to think these things with, to feel these places with. And so, I go, go back, and so?

Can this be an Irish poem?

When we first met, walking the dark, back
from a pub, Craig said, 'I made an Irish library
in my head and called it home.'
We spoke of being frauds. 'To work in words
I had to leave,' I told him.

'Forty years of weighing Ireland.'

What will we find beside the Bann,
inside the Bann, beside each other,

inside ourselves?

How else to take the North

of surnames, legends, photographs,

make a frame big enough

for London to stand in?

In Belfast, before our train on to Bangor, we run into The Crown for the swiftest of drinks. Tucked into an ornate and wood-dark booth, we take down the cold black stuff.

'How this place escaped the Troubles...,' Cherry says, looking up at the ceiling and the Victorian stained glass that covers the inside with a chocolatey pall.

There's a sense of sloughing off something like responsibility, though in truth, a journey like this only substitutes of one set of responsibilities for another.

'You'll have to help me,' she says as she stands, pointing to the creamy dregs of her pint.

At Bangor, Cherry meets a smiling man with the languid ease of an old friend. This is Peter, who is tall and milk-mild with only the faintest of flecks of Ulster in his voice. People always think he's English, both here and in England, where he's lived much of his life. In a Volvo estate as old as me, they discuss the town. Peter says that Bangor has huge potential, but he knows nothing will happen here, nothing will change.

'You know who are in charge,' is his explanation.

'This is the land I came back for,' says Peter

my Islington neighbour of three decades, who's

settled back in Ballyholme, 'not hedges and lawns and
                                                    blocked drains.'

Welcome to Newry, Mourne and Down, where

an *Iúir, Mhúrn, agus an Dúin* are scratched out

at the metal edge of the tongue's border.

Peter is our Boircha, the herdsman who leads us

up Bog Road, along Fofanny Road to Spelga Dam.

Spelga was sweetened yoghurt not *speilgeach*,

place of pointed rocks. One pot, one lunch,

my anorexic will, eating Irish all those teenage years,

unaware of its source.

What we call the source of a river is more or less, arbitrary. The Bann begins in a high muddy field, hidden and diffused in countless rills and trickles. But then, something pools in me. I realise I've been here before. A trip. *Her* last trip. We took her over the Mournes, to the coast. We took this road, we passed this field.

And now I push something away. That journey was not meant to meet this one. The unfamiliar was not meant to become familiar. Memory is a high muddy field, its source hidden and diffused.

Skylarks spark off the slope

    that gives us pyramid orchids.

The trickster source

    is stowed

        in the sphagnum moss,

           a vivid, deceptive sponge

           that soaks up five streams

              of a stony star.

Is this it?

Where is the sky-reflecting bauble I have dreamt?

Craig claims it to the east,

        me, further north.

    The mountain is releasing secret rains

    and we're apprentices in origins,

    can't read the incline signs.

And why is it that this trickle on a hill leading down to the dam is the Bann, and not another? And why is the water leaving the dam called the Bann? Why not some other?

This is the question: What causes a river to be named and tracked through the landscape? Naming is an attempt to gather things, that might not be the same, together. Bloodline and family. People and nations.

Beyond the dam, the long-limbed *an Bhanna*,
the Goddess, takes her rise, her feet fresh, her mind
digressive, defining her own route to North Terminal,
where her world opens into all worlds, the Barmouth.
The true source hangs in cloud above Deer's Meadow,
recalling salt. I want to know its circular transfixion,
sun-steam from sea, fall to ground, breathing rain.

Looking for the source,
startle yellow asphodels –
heart beats in the feet.

Already we're on the road, walking fast and even
below two peaks, Cock and Hen. I am a chickling dot
moving along the summit sling that dips symmetrical
as an arc inked in Zen. As I swing up my rucksack,
my body is eighteen, the ferry leaving Piraeus for Ios,
Paros, Naxos and Santorini. I am strong, self-sufficient,
my legs young, hips skipping nicely. Craig is impressed.
I have over twenty years more road in me.

For months, I touched the Goddess via
fluorescent high-lighter, and now its slender strone

over rocks below the road, is muted, droughtish.

Climate // panic // flashes // through // me!

Can this be the river – can this be the river's future? –

the broad, deep, childhood river that transported

coal to Coleraine?

Because I am a son of the map, a son of the wide-view, the abstraction, my family tree is painted on parchment, not in the bricks of the Big House, the thatch of some bedewed cottage or on a Falls Road mural.

The real world is filled with avenues of blood and water. Sometimes we call them rivers, sometimes we call them borders. Some rivers are as thick as blood, some borders, as thick as water. These avenues are always, in the final instance, stories.

I want significance, not this remnant lost to a reservoir

that wets and washes Portadown and Banbridge.

I persuade Craig to streel off course to touch Finn's

Fingerstone, fifty tons of buttery granite, aslant tumbled

trestles. We snack in the deep quietness of three ash

in a grassy hollow, a sacred green, recently mowed.

This is a place to begin, a portal

to that other hub where all river-walkers go.

It took Finn McCool one finger to toss the capstone

and create the dam. Last week Loyalists drove

golf balls across the line into Catholic windows.

They   want   the   strength   of   giants.

The English are noted for being passive-aggressive. In Northern Ireland, I've not found passive-aggression, but I've found passivity *and* aggression. The aggression's there in the flags, the bunting, the bonfires with hated names burning, the signs to repent, and the slogans never to surrender, the graffiti for the U.D.A/R.I.R.A, where the Irish never forget, and the English never remember. At least, I think, I'm not the only one still trying too hard.

But then, it's not all murals, marches and memorials. Discounting the shrillness of callers to radio phone-ins, there can be a studied reticence about identity, at least when you don't know who you're talking to. Is this a shyness? A politeness? Whatever it is, it's hardly new. There's an old path here that's been paved with oblique questions: How do you spell your name? What school did you go to? Who's your Da? Where are you from? People knew the game, and knew when it was being played.

You know who, were in charge.

Can this be an Irish place?

Up the hemmed Ballynagappoge Road towards Clonduff,

cow parsley and honeysuckle buzz in white and lemon.

Craig spots a twitch of brown air at the roadside,

a wren juking in out of sight. He calls it the jizz,

a birder's eye. A harvester fills the road with noise

and leaves a wake of hay and diesel. And another.

And a tractor with a trailer full of rattle. Fatter plant

will widen these skinny roads. Satellite boulders

from the dolmen serve as gate posts or garden design.

They say it's bad luck to disturb a fairy grave.

Katesbridge to Banbridge

Give me Compeed, the pilgrim's plaster.

The feet's story has begun: the sorry rub of sixteen miles.

I channel pressure to the instep, the heel, anywhere

but the toes.

My pack has doubled in weight. I decant stuff to Craig's back.

Later, he'll take what the walk will unfold from the

family hotpress -

heavy linen, old beach towels that present the hands' work,

both wanted and unwanted, under warm order.

'The map is a shield,' he says but it shows no river path

at Katesbridge. Margaret comes to our aid, points past

the abandoned railway, the renovated schoolhouse,

'Go through my ground to the left corner. If anyone says

anything, just say Margaret said it was OK.'

She steps out of an album of the dead – two sisters who

ran the shop, the linen mill workers, the Kate who offered

tea to the builders of the handsome, arched bridge.

Yesterday, men healing walls and weather-proofing fences,

only grunted. We are thirsty for Margaret.

'It's very cold here, a frost hollow,' she says. 'Minus 18

in the winter. And lonely.' Cancer took her husband last year.

And many years before, girls would wash their clothes

in the river. One time, an eerie wailing made them gather up their laundry and rush home. One girl, hunkered at the water, heard nothing. Later they learnt she'd drowned.

Whoever doesn't hear the banshee, is about to die.

This too, is a place to begin.

The walk is around ten miles to Banbridge town, where my family are from. My grandad came to England during the war, dug out Blitz-buried bodies and then, like many Irish immigrants, worked Britain's building sites. Not so much of a brain-drain, as a brawn-drain, some say. And like many Irish immigrants, he would travel back, bring his children back, create the stories and the sources I, too-keen, still pursue today.

Today, we will wade through pooled patches of nettles, bare arms aloft. We will hold out those arms to one another as handrails and crutches as we swing over stiles and wobble over fences. This is the hearty stuff I had imagined. We are not just on our way to Banbridge, it feels like we are on our way to the Atlantic. But every few fields there is a mucky runway down to the river, where the cattle head to drink. To stop them entering the water, each path is barred with a double gate, under which the edges of the Bann gather. This doesn't always work. In one field the wooden posts have decayed and gates like drunken staves slump into the water. We see half a dozen cows hoof-deep, played on by dappled light. They drop their heads down, gullets pulsing as they take up the cool Bann. Yes, this is the hearty stuff I had imagined. That is, until they lift their tails and shit fountains into the water.

The Bann is shallow, lane-narrow. The eye leans

across it, sometimes favouring fat blue, then flat green.

We meet no one on the anglers' path, can't utter
                                    Margaret's password.

On low branches, traces of spate mat into dark wigs.

Weeds are the capes the river first wore.

A froth of white flowers floats downriver. Pipes sneak in,

carrying run-off. The crowsfoot will die if slurried too much.

If the river is hidden, so is what enters it.

Cherry becomes attuned to the different kinds of muck and shite that dance about the air in great sultry wafts. 'Smells like pig,' she says of the airslurry around a concrete shed near Gilford. 'Ah, that's cow,' she will note, as a breeze blows down off the high fields of Bendooragh.

I wonder about a cartographic possibility. A mid-Ulster map of smells, cut through with tones of brown and tan, flexing over the landscape. As well as borders drawn by county and constituency, and borders etched by river and mountain, there would also be borders of the air: County Muck, Slieve Slurry, West Nosefast. These places would never settle and everyone would have to accept they could not hold down the provinces of the air.

The cow smell is heavy and mouldy; pig smell,

acrid and high; the poultry, rotting shells and seaweed.

Everywhere the whiff of shite. And where to put it?

Norfolk? Wexford? Agri-business is too big for its shit.

We swipe off sticky clegs. The Goddess is wailing

and no one can hear.

Outside Banbridge, the soft day never wakes up.

It's a day to let sadness silt. We hack back nettle corridors,

climb buried stiles, crawl under fences to avoid
                                                    electrocution.

Recreating a lost path makes a bond that beats eco-anxiety

for a while. A ship's hull looms from the opposite bank,

with rigging and a pulley like some outdoor stage –
                                a punk performance? –

but it's a Game of Thrones Centre, bankrolling new myths.

The path stops. Craig strides up a meadow trembling with

cornflowers, buttercup, goldenrod. I want to keep
                                Bann-close

beyond a birch wood. I plough through yarrow, white clover,

red clover, a knapweed haugh. I only remember knapweed

because I drew it when I learnt its name, and the drawing

gave me longer looking than the word could...I hit
                                barbed wire.

Craig calls 'Hey!'... He's found a path! I give in,

I promise to keep giving in.

The foot. The feet. The folding of the path up into yourself.
You can feel the furrows and fields in your limbs, hear the
car rush and truck rush and the rattling metal in that buzzing
place beyond hearing. Sometimes before sleep, you still hear
the hiss of the world cycling in you.

Two silos poxed with rust

sculpt the field, offset

the barn, telling us that we've backed

round on ourselves, brambled and

briared out of river access.

I huff, puff and resent

each retraced step.

This is the pilgrim's lesson.

A circle is as good as a straight line.

The map is remade in losing it.

We will hold out arms where the edges of the Bann gather.

It was Wordsworth who invented the term 'pedestrian', from the Latin for foot, *pes*. Simply put, a pedestrian was someone who went by foot. Today, we use it to mean something is unremarkable, expected. Though our daily meanings hide histories and are rarely pedestrian. Wordsworth coined the term at a time when walking was an act of necessity for most. But the Romantics, with their loftier goals and inward eyes, were not satisfied by being mere walkers. No, they were not walkers, but pedestrians. A pedestrian walked from choice, not necessity. So, the Romantic pedestrian is anything but pedestrian.

And the pompous and ponderous footfall of the Romantics is important to remember, because as we travel along this river, we can forget that travel itself always speaks. A dinghy heading toward Dover, overflowing with people and sea, speaks. A flight from Gatwick to Belfast without the need for passports, speaks. The liners squeezing into Venice like an arse into jeans, speaks. And two writers walking the Bann, speaks. The task then, is to hear what it says.

Miles of road later.

Only water can soothe me.

Craig wants to press on. I plead.

We strip off, crouch down a mucky cleavage

to the river. My hot feet hiss. My legs come.

You could barely call it swimming.
The water is shallow and sluggish,
its furry rocks hibernating in the tabby light.
Cool gives us three more miles.

Harry's Bar has the best seats in the world, the tastiest
beer, the crispiest crisps. We've stepped out
of Covid and have to step back in, mask up. Sign in.
Our certificate for reaching a pilgrim's stage-post
is a test and trace requirement. My shoulders take off
in elastic elation, a great grin of accomplishment
on Tayto lips. The bunting seems jaunty. It can be cultural.

Warm evening Banbridge.
Solitude Park is heaving.
We carry the miles.

Banbridge to Portadown

Day 3 begins in a car. The Compeed has melted
to a gesso cushion on the blisters like artificial skin.
I waver between being a tourist and a local, emigrant
and anthropologist, trying to be open to what each
skin can let in. Or keeps out. We pass a sculpture cut
to the course of a cobalt Bann, its steel surface
used for stickers for gigs. Is this where mussels
thickened in blue-black clusters, their lustrous hubs
plucked and shucked for pearls sold in London?
Or where May bloomed a flax tide of blue,
each flower fresh for a day, before the stalks splayed
and stank out the fields?

We drive up a steep hill, to where Craig's great
grandfather, Sean Jordan lived. Aka the Professor,
he fixed bikes, started clocks and lived in a terrace
near the railway bridge. All that's left is a hedge
and a shining field: his view. No story without Aunt
Kate's pride in the man who could cycle these hills.

When I came to Banbridge as a kid, I would stay with Aunt
Kate, as we do now. Her house was always immaculate and
she was always immaculate. She still is, with the polish and

poise of a First Lady. But today Kate has loops unclosed, has had her sources taken from her. Since we last saw each other, her only child Shane, has died. On the green slope of Banbridge cemetery, he has joined her husband, Steve. And with Steve, there's another story, one I'm still not sure if I have a right to tell.

Steve Carroll was a Catholic born in the Republic, brought up in England, who then moved to the North. A sportsman, an RUC man, then a PSNI man, I remember how his English tones were channelled with Ulster notes. He was a true amalgam. Back in 2009, he was called out to investigate a robbery, which wasn't a robbery at all. A sniper shot. Then not long after, a knock on my aunt Kate's immaculate door. Those uniforms and the grim faces told her everything.

Now, Steve is everywhere in the house. Not just in the photos that line Kate's tables and climb her walls, but in the way my memory seeks him out in this space. When I met him, I was a body-conscious fourteen-year-old. He owned a bench press, was super-trim and broad-shouldered. He showed me how to lift, how to make your arms, not your back, do the work. Back then, Steve was the kind of shape I wanted to shape myself into.

'In my line of work, it pays to be fit,' he said.

No amount of fitness can stop a bullet. And looking back, that possibility threaded his life, both their lives. It was understood I wasn't to mention his job outside of the house. I soon learned that like all cops in the North, Steve didn't work where he lived. Otherwise, you might be identified; get a bullet as you shopped, walked your dog, ate a meal.

As he left for work one morning, I remember glimpsing a gun tucked against his ribs as he shucked on his jacket. It was the first I had ever seen. I knew there were guns, too many guns, in the North, but I felt embarrassed by how much it frightened me. Steve turned away to kiss Kate goodbye. He didn't acknowledge my gaze, never offered to show me the weapon, never mentioned it. It made me doubt if the shape of his life was the shape I wanted for my own.

And now after a hard day of walking, I'm coming out of the shower at Kate's, and feel another tumble of memory. My mother. Standing there dripping, I remember this was the cubicle where I showered her. She was scared that she would trip on the lip, and I had to use all my strength to balance and support her, all the time pretending I wasn't scared she would fall. I can hear her breath, heavy.

Kate's house is cream and silver in every room,

with statues of women in long cream dresses.

It is a temple to Aphrodite, a shrine to the love she lost,

a man shot at work, answering a night call. The evening

windows fill with midsummer sun, not gold enough to

displace the sorrow, twelve years old, and start her clocks.

On the final day of one Banbridge trip, Steve gave me a set of dumbbells. They were 8kg apiece, cobalt-blue and I was thrilled. He said he didn't need them, though the fact I mentioned how meagre my pocket money was might have made a difference.

Too keen as usual, I enthusiastically lugged my manly merchandise through Belfast City Airport. At security, of course, my bag was flagged, separated. A uniformed man with deadened eyes waved me over.

'Can you tell me what's in the bag, please?'

I paused, for too long.

'Dumbbells,' I said, though I probably stuttered. It was occurring to me that carrying 16kg of body-building equipment through an airport during the Troubles might have raised suspicions. The security guard scanned my face. Was this kid taking the piss or was he just stupid?

The bag was opened and my cobalt cargo was hauled out. The guard paused, for too long. He glared at me, at them, at me, weighing my scrawny stupidity.

'On your way now,' he said as his mouth failed to pin down his smirk.

Behind the leisure centre, the river's skin has the slow

metabolic pulse of rolling glass. Its banks tell the town:

Tesco bags and Tennents cans, signs for suicide helplines.

We pause along flat, riparian fields, listening to reeds sift

the damage of dung, of chemical slayers and boosters.

Just to prove you are human, find the future in these pictures.

A few days in now and the journey starts to take on shape not of individual roads or boreens, not of particular scenes or places, but of something more tapestried. We begin to live in a world of hedge and road, gleaming, drab houses and sundered outbuildings. It is a world of water and walking that shifts and tacks when I try to bring it into focus, try to tell you what it really is.

And this too, is what the imagination does when we travel. It wrestles the small things into something we can hold up and say, 'the people here are so hospitable', 'the weather is like this'. And so many of those submerged smallnesses of hillglide and footscupper will never be thought about.

We, alone, walk the road.

Poor people walk, refugees walk,

the homeless walk.

This is not leisure or work.

It is walking into writing, pulling

words from the river and the road.

It is walking into time,

into imagination's step,

where our ancestors walked.

Another tributary of talk bubbles up,

eats the distance, how I dreamed out,

how Craig dreamed over.

On a nameless road hedged between the day's start and end,

it begins to rain. First a fug of swaying, tiny droplets, and then something more like downpour. We put on our macs as the smell of muck leaps into the air. We expect a soaking, but the rain lasts only minutes.

Can this be an Irish poem?

I realise now that if the rain had continued and we had trudged for wet hours, this moment would have been washed away. Because memory, along with everything else, is not watertight.

At Tullylish, a lush sward tilts over a hill, once a bleaching

green. A small round tower, with a beehive lid, the lookout.

A watchman watched the linen take on the moonlight, spread

and stiffen its white plate. Thieves, fox-soft, waited for cloud,

a wane, risked death or down under, if caught.

I lie down, eat nuts and drink, drink, drink.

We've no hunger: the body suspects lack, tucks

into reserves. What of those with no home ahead,
                                              no phone,

no belongings, a continent in their soles, ruins in their eyes?

I heave to stand. This chosen hardship strikes me
                                              as obscene.

Craig lifts my pack and I strap in, stooping in a future age.

The sharp joists of my legs pivot into the roof of my hips.

I am deconstructing home, bricks at my ankles,

a full hod on each shoulder, a blister as large as a toe.

Tullylish used to thrum with scutching, spinning
                                                        and weaving.

England scuppered Ireland's linen trade to boost

its own. We leave the Hillock of the Fort with no fort, no mills,

only a church, a graveyard and an empty watchhouse.

A day where our feet are at their sorest. As we trudge and grind the journey's romance into the grit we feel far from Wordsworth's pedestrians. We turn, take up the path beside the Newry canal. 'U.V.F' is sprayed, black and angular and repeated every few hundred metres, for around a mile. Dogs do this, they lift their legs and spurt out a yellow streak on whatever feels theirs. It fills the air with threat, this piss, but Cherry doesn't notice. We pause where the Canal meets the river and look east. Less than a mile away, a low-slung and humpy town addles the skyline. We have arrived in Portadown.

Let's not be coy: in Portadown, mediocrity squints at you through the bluster of High Street bunting. It creeps up through grey flagstones, dangles from flaccid flags. Portadown is not unlike other towns, where ugliness and utility share the same toothbrush, but there's something here that feels different. It feels, well, Portadown.

Bannview is full for the 12th

and we're the uninvited.

John texts me: 'Give Portadown

a kiss and a kick from me. If you want

instant depression, walk along

Obins Street to Drumcree.

A hard-faced place.'

At the Bannview B&B, you might expect, without overt optimism, a Bann view. Our room overlooks the river, or at least it would. Across the road, a sour, redbrick box with a giant, plastic 'Family Cafe' sign, blocks out the water. Bannview replaced by Brickview. It's like there's some Portadownish insistence that the river, reed-lined and heron-rich, shall not be noticed.

Craig says that Northern Ireland

is an abused child, unwanted by its parents.

Nowhere have I felt it more.

Kinship thrives here in details lost to hectic

roads and roundabouts, a backend coming first.

I lance my blisters and hope I'll sleep.

A dream of L. creases me.

Walking can't iron it.

I need steamy sex.

This town is a station on the pilgrimage, and as necessary as anywhere else. And by now I know that beauty and perfect connection are things I would easily tire of. And it's in Portadown that I add a word to the annals of human emotion.

Are you feeling down?

No, I'm feeling Portadown.

Portadown

to Bannfoot

The Bann is a wide and deep overcast mirror of slate.

We zigzag in a double canoe, the Divorce Boat,

says the instructor, Steve. We take a while to dance

with the current, matching a change in movement

and environment. 'If he goes in, you go in'.

A heron lifts its tatty grey heap and right-angles into the sky.

Craig follows with his bins. Cars hurtle over the bridge

from Craigavon. A motorboat passes. Three portly men laugh

at our riverine progress. We laugh back from the Stone Age.

'Don't go in a canoe if you don't want to get wet,' says Steve.

Like age, I think, 'Don't live in a body if you can't face getting old.'

Nothing is watertight, we can only slow its entry.

There are the stories we can't tell all at once, the stories that build like sediment. Sometimes, this is because of shame, and our throats close before the story is opened. And sometimes, this is because we don't know what the story is yet.

The story of my mother's death is like this. As we walk, it is touched on and stepped over and hinted at. The cancer. The care home. The final trip to see family in Banbridge. Cherry knows by the gaps, the difficulty of this story. But why is it difficult, just to say, to share as we heave against the miles that prop up the Bann's banks? Because, I realise, this is a story about not knowing.

I did not know how painful even a pill-filled death could be.

How the dying cry out for their mothers, cry out for help, for hours and hours. Then later, when the morphine finally tightens a gauze around their world, how drug-stifled cries puff from them, how lungs filling with fluid make her breath sound like the creaking and clacking of winter trees. How even with her son near, she is alone. There is no mother for my mother, no friend, no son. This story is hard to paint onto the shifting sky, the shifting water.

But we have time, don't we?

Yes, we have time.

> The paddles slip in quiet
>
> and jibble sound
>
> as they come out, ringing
>
> to lilies at the banks,
>
> the stupas of rosebay willow herb.
>
> Fish jump and thump the surface.
>
> Demoiselles blip by
>
> in sapphire glints.
>
> We arrow through Scots Pine,
>
> oak, alder and elm
>
> meeting themselves in the water.
>
> We are also doubled, but can't see
>
> how we float on mottled clouds.
>
> Travelling up the river's spine,

we become direct movement north,

nose where the Bann noses,

on the line, not next to it,

awake in the dream, not dreaming it,

our yellow paddles and red lifejackets,

like touches of bright clothing in a Corot

landscape, signalling consciousness.

Pilgrimage is nothing if not taking time,

making the path the clock.

The present presses all future

into today's miles, the alluvium of grief,

of city, of work, left in water's passing.

What hunger pulls us towards the mouth? The mouth of conversation. The mouth of poetry. The mouth of song. The mouth of inquiry. The mouth of question. The open mouth, the closed mouth, the dry mouth, the full mouth, mouth of the river, of the tunnel, the cave, valley. A salmon's mouth popping on the river, a friend's mouth pursing to kiss.

Being on the water, the Bloody Bridge behind us,

I wonder why I'd never heard about

the hundred Protestants thrown into the river,

shot till they stilled, in a tumult of trophy or tragedy

in 1641, that roiled into centuries. As if on

the River Jordan, Israeli flags fly in East Belfast.

British history favoured the terra nullius

of the Plantation as if the Irish didn't exist.

My heart streams the Scottish ancestors who came

as settlers, but also beats for the young workman,

waiting at a roundabout, around here, for a lift,

his dawn movements known, picked out by a bullet

marked 'Catholic'. So much to file under 'Ancient Battles',

'Recent Killings', with more weariness than healing.

It's paddles we're using, not oars.

'Oars propel you away from the direction you're facing, whereas paddles push you the way you're facing,' our instructor Steve pointed out back in Portadown. Whatever the distinction, the word 'oar', with its great yawning vowel, is what I'd have preferred. There's languid ease in 'oar', whereas 'paddle' has only a fiddly indecision.

But that turns out to be appropriate as we fiddle our way along the water. Our paddles were meant to glide into silk waters as we, cygnine, slipped towards Lough Neagh. Eventually, we pull into something like a rhythm, something like a purposeful line. But like language, the boat is harder to control than I would have thought. Like thought is.

Mum would get so tired she would fall from the chair, if you weren't there to stop her. Like a child, she would deny she had been asleep, even as her chin and forehead drooped towards the thick glass of Kate's kitchen table.

When we were visiting a cousin, Mum got too hot, asked if she could take off her headscarf. In that small, muggy room she unwrapped the scarf, leaving a skullcap of cancer, red and foamy and prickled with hairs that broke its livery surface. Packed tight, I heard the quietness of polite shock around her: continue to talk about the weather, or Uncle Eddie or what we're up to tomorrow. Don't look, and don't don't look.

A few months later and, impossible to control, those tumours grew to a monstrous extent (I hate that word, an ugly word, a word that shouldn't belong to her. But it does.) Bulging and dripping down the blood vessels of her face, the tumours soon covered her eyes, left her blind.

I want oars, not paddles. I want to face *away* from my direction of thought.

'Do your family sing?' Craig asks.

'Oh yes, a lot. The first two lines of many

songs. Then we falter into dum-dee-dum.'

He starts singing with buccaneer gusto:

'In Banbridge town, in the County Down,

one morning last July,

from a boreen green came a sweet colleen

and she smiled as she passed me by....'

I join in, in bits. I didn't grow up with Rosie McCann.
I sing the blues Dad taught on the road to school:
'This is the story of a most unfortunate coloured man
who was 'rrested down in old Hong Kong.
He got forty years' privilege taken away from him
when he beat old Buddha's gong.'

I'm more Hoagy Carmichael and the Ink Spots
than The Chieftains and Planxty but the tang
of lament flavours what we each sing to the jaup
of the Bann. My dad lingers, not here, not gone.
'I don't want you to see me like this,' he said when
his memory began to shrink as he spoke.

What makes us sing for the first time?
The more open sky, the slow rhythmic strokes,
being a crew, the audience of the water and the
languor in the windless air. Is it the same thing
that convinced Craig to take the river through a homeland
he can't quite claim and I can't quite renounce?
Perhaps if I accept I've left for good, something
will bring me back: water-curved light,
the daughtering voice of earth that grew me.

Or will simply having thought this,

cancel fate's magical inversion?

> At canoe dock
>
> on Heron Boulevard
>
> ideas wind a rope bobbin.

Bannfoot to Toome

We are dropped off by taxi to Kinnego Marina, on the shores of Lough Neagh. The haze of distance and what look like headlands sloping out from the west would convince many this was a sea. Beyond a gaggle of white yachts and boats that gird the gangways, the water is wide, silken. We will be taken over the lough by an old eel fisherman named Frankie, who works on the water, part steward, part police.

We walk down a gangway, eyeing a bent figure gathering rope. The figure straightens; a broad, red-faced man who waves with a certainty rarely seen in strangers. Clearly, we are the strangers here.

Soon we feel the lull of Neagh beneath us, a secret gravity. The boat - small, clean and searing white, is not what I expected. Somehow, I expected rust and winches and bad weather and I catch myself again, laugh a little inward.

The belly of the Goddess laps five counties.

(Fermanagh has plenty of water of its own.)

Plantation names like Lough Sydney and Chichester

didn't stick. The Lough spreads its sky, shifting

silver elongations and summer blue into navy.

The surface tells of depth, something metallic

and dull you think you can hear. Frankie has kind,

blue eyes, a protruding lower lip and a soft voice.

'The water has no friends,' his dad warned him. Few

want to get up predawn, face the shabby weather.

The lough is an isogloss, making the accent more
sleepy, less jagged as we travel north. The sound
is cosy, more 'culchie' we would say. (Turns out,
I was a culchie and didn't know it.) From *coillte*,
Irish for woods – we didn't know it, eating Irish
all those teenage years, unaware of its source.

We're learning where Irish and English meet,
rub along against each other, scratched out
at the metal edge of the tongue's border.

A wheen of elver fattens below us, turning argent.
Readying for autumn, they will starve, seal their anus,
burn flesh-fuel. One moonless, blustery night,
they'll point one heart north, swim out through Toome,
the tail-heart letting go of their adolescent home.

Clever, non-binary eels, you adapt to lack. Too many
and you become male, not enough – female.
The sea's mantra pulls you north – *Sargasso* – then
south – *Sargasso* – as far as the Canaries – then west –
Sargasso – to spawn and die. Six thousand kilometres,
twice, with Lough Neagh, your life's fulcrum.

Frankie tells us less come, less leave. Overfished,

overheated, over-polluted, their cycle thins.

Elvers are bought from the Netherlands.

Accidental zebra mussels are sucking up

the fishes' food. Less chemicals enter but

the danger keeps coming out of the bedrock.

Being here and talking to Frankie makes me recall an eight-hundred-year-old book, *Topographia Hibernica* by Gerald of Wales. Gerald travelled around Ireland, then the frontier of the Anglo-Norman empire, to write what he heard and saw. He wrote of a freakish land where birds flew upside down and where some oxen were half-men, some men half-ox. His main aim seems to have been to convince the reader that the Irish were a violent, lazy and barbarous people. It's the classic colonial strategy. He even provides a picture of a woman in foreplay with a goat. But Gerald can't stifle his respect when he describes Neagh and the river that leaves it.

There is a lake in Ulster of a remarkable size. It is thirty miles long and fifteen miles wide. From it a very beautiful river called the Bann flows through to the northern ocean. Here the fishermen complain not of the scarcity of fish, but of too great catches and the breaking of their nets.

But now, scarcity is the complaint. We quiz Frankie on many things: his background, Brexit, the life cycle of the eel, the weather, the sand dredged by ever larger and more sophisticated ships. The term 'extraction' rises up to meet us: extraction of sand, clay, salmon, eel. The dredging up of an Iron Age disc, a Viking shield grip, tools of dark flint. The water has been a source of wealth: clay was cut for the brickworks at Toome, sand sifted for roadmaking, building.

Frankie has specific terms for the water: Milk (calm), Rip (very bad) and Dirty (twice as bad). Today, we are lucky. But the water has no friends. I cannot but accept the heavyfast truth. Of course the water has no friends. It is the water. It does not care and more than this, it does not not care. The indifference is absolute.

Today's lough is not milk, more of an undulating dim

and bright silk that, Frankie cautions, could turn.

Jet-skiers have been caught out, canoeists stranded.

More than one fisherman vanished over the prow

without a sound. No whistling if you don't want

a storm; no smoking if you want to charm the fish.

Ardboe Abbey and Slieve Gullion are our lodestars,

but Frankie knows each benthic constellation: Silver Hill,

Summer Flat, Oul Hole, Chelsea Flat – the gravel beds,

the rocky mounts, the clay stretches, the robbed sand

that disturbs the spawning. Family names for each substrate

hump and hollow prove as accurate as any echo sounder.

He ignores the screen fluorescents guiding his path, outlining
the catch of dollaghan, perch, pike, pollan and roach.

The water has no friends...

There's a story about the stretch of water leading into Toome.
It's called, 'the run': a narrow, deeply cut avenue in the lough
bed. Some say this means that once, the Upper and Lower
Banns were one.

This dream could make sense of separation, of that frailty
in naming the two Banns. In this dream, the Bann exists before
Neagh, and in spate, breaking its banks, would have birthed
the lough.

The septic tank of the North, Frankie calls it.

We've ruined all but one of Ulster's twenty-five lakes.

No matter how many times I read this,

I can't lodge hypertrophic knowing in my bones.

The fear of what's to come runs off my surface.

Lion's Brow: the diesel churns.

White Horse Flat: the water plumps.

Buck Rock rises feverishly.

Ram's Island: blood leaves my head.

Nanny's mud: the lough spins.

I hit Connolly's Hard.

It happens like a sweet, sickly sleep,

  falling a level too deep, without a sound,

    waking flat out on deck to a brighter brightness,

      to Frankie kneeling, Craig talking first aid to someone

        who doesn't know my name. She yearns to touch land

          and be motionless. Some border has been crossed.

How many words between us? How many steps on the road? How much hedge trimming the fields? How many clouds gauzing the sky? How much sand dredged from Lough Neagh? How much rain squeezed from the hills into the Bann? How can a field of trickles end in an ocean?

I keep my eyes on the carry of the sky, let the swirl settle,

re-house the drifted spirit. The water has new menace.

I stay with the deck's fresh white paint and sealed chests,

as if inside Frankie's medicine cabinet.

There were no ideas, no conclusions in coming

round in a clean O of painless sound. When I
was away, they guarded what I couldn't
in that dark silence, next to darkest.

Wouldn't death be the same, with no waking
and no knowledge of being asleep? Face shapeless,
limbs a flop, who was I, where was I? If Craig
hadn't noticed the swivel in my gaze, hadn't levered

me down, I could have toppled overboard,
without a sound, been taken to the river's heart.
I can't know but I knew I had been beyond
only when I returned and I was glad to be back.

We are halfway.

Toome to Portglenone

Ferried over the Styx, we land at Toome. A tricolour
frays from a lamppost. A black flag next to a photo
I half recognise. A handsome young man, with black

hair, thick eyebrows, a cared-for handlebar moustache.
It's the 40th anniversary of the Hunger Strike and we didn't
keep count. Craig wasn't born. I was twenty-one when
he died.

Kevin Lynch. It's his engagement photo. I marched
in the rain down O'Connell Street. I didn't know which way
to turn. I entered history through another door,

in step with other students, all generations,
a mourning protest that closed the shame on bystanding.
He could have been a father, a grandfather,

a first minister, a peace leader. Like the salmon
and the eel, he followed instinct running
through his DNA, living off his own volition

for seventy-one days. Ten young men,

their jaws kype-like, no fight left,

crossed the border without a sound.

We will hold out arms where the edges of the Bann gather.

To say that the river is just a river or that this piece of land is just land seeks reduction: just a pile of rock, an old tree, a hill, a flag, a colour, a date. In a place like this, a place with a history of violence, it's obvious we would wish for 'just'.

When space itself is contested, it's a kind of resistance to pay less attention to it. Things are just what they are, and no more. To say the river is just the river shields you from the strange ways the land and water transform when we begin to see ourselves in them.

But the river is not just a river, and land is not just land. There is always an 'and' in Northern Ireland.

This is a rock and the place where they...

This is a hill and used to be...

Where 'and' is, space gains weight. Where 'and' is, space becomes place.

Can this be an Irish poem? An Irish space?

Smell guides salmon to their home river. We are severed
east of the Bann, with no sight or scent of it.

Just as river is eclipsed by sea, the Goddess waits
in the shadow of the bright appetite of greed.

I disbelieve in Goddess but want
the ancient system's strength in such belief.

I've been taught a subtle shunning
of anything feminine with power.

How far back, *An Bhanna*, must I travel
to enter memory of your worship,

to understand the holy
that christened you, pre-Christ,

the shrines and wells that drew the festivals
of cure, the palm-warmed offerings?

You lost out to Cú Chulainn's war dogs
and the might of Finn McCool, churched

in rumour, then neglected: the damage

from the lapse in care cannot be undone.

Throughout our journey, I've been reading another journey. Before I left, I squeezed a copy of *The Táin* into my pack, Ireland's answer to *The Odyssey*. I hoped that the handrails of the past, of myth, might make the Bann glitter a little more, might thicken the line of the present into something broader than bankside and roadside. So, I scan for Donn Cuailnge snorting through a hawthorn window; I feel the warp spasm of traffic on Loughbeg Road; on my pillow at the B&B, I read the Pillow Talk.

This is a kind of tourism I realise I've been practising much of my life. It's a consequence of always dreaming over. But the relation is thin, the Pangs of Ulster are different today. The Ulster Cycle is more an old bike shop in Portadown than a body of legend. I've not lived on the land, but alongside it, in a kind of anteroom. In that room, I've heard the sound dulled through walls and echoed down long halls.

We tread a pavement, a verge, pebble-dashed

between low walls. Traffic comes in swarms,

logistics lorries spewing dust, harvesters spraying hay.

'This is boring,' says Craig. Who else could I have coaxed

along a river you can't see, through trim, prim countryside,

marked by the austere opulence of homes?

We reckon with a hollow gunk, miss the heron,
                                                    miss the mission.

Water gave us direction, now it's duty. Pinched

and Prodded, we pass another Orange Hall, a red sign

on a pole: 'It is time to seek the Lord Jesus.'

Our steps say home, what home, at home, not home, away

home, play home, fuck home, deny home, rely home,
                                                    cry home.

Slow down...focus on the tarmac textures:

the pale pink flecks like fresh bubblegum;

the gravel that grinds blisters; the red warning

at a T-junction saying YIELD, tyre-worn

into atolls of wordless coral.

Handbrake turns have spun interlocking loops

across the road, as minimal

as a Brice Marden monochrome.

I miss New York, the sanctity of galleries,

the smart, spatial buzz and belonging.

I scan the horizon for a modernist line,

walk through the broken letters of YIELD.

Our sentimentality toward rivers belies the fact we often ignore them when our lives happen near them. They look so real and definite from the sky, on the map, in the imagination. In those spaces, the blue ribbon of the Bann, the Goddess, is always in spate with promise.

Though in Portglenone, or in Banbridge, in Toome, you ask about the river and receive a shrug, even surprise. It is just a river. We ask a writer, a business owner, relatives, who frown, have little to say. We interview a biologist who says she didn't notice the Bann before her work forced her attention on it. And if you asked me about my home river, the Itchen, I would frown and say it's just a river.

Because a river is whole only when seen on the map. The map smooths out the edges of reality to allow the possibility, the fiction, of seeing clearly. But we do not see clearly. We see that slice of water under that bridge, that cross-section on our commute. So how could we expect anything else from those we've talked to? After all, it's Cherry and I who are trying to build clarity here, wrestle our fiction into reality.

We have taken down the map and pressed it, pushed it, into the earth and water.

We accept all this: the thin promises, the abstraction, the fiction of this pilgrimage. And yet we still need to gather something together. Because the river may be hidden, but it does not need to be.

We vigil walk. We vigil talk.

When a river is hidden so is what enters it.

In law, in Bangladesh, rivers are people.

But women are not always people.

Who protects us from the protectors?

Before long the Goddess will be fetid,

disenchanting, another dead zone,

craving a phosphate fix, a nitrate high.

We'll find new ways to bury the poison fire.

The moon is on her back. I see nothing

but black water. Whoever doesn't hear

the banshee will surely die.

Ah, the old once-upon-a-time. The gilded long-ago. The stories we are told and tell ourselves, about blood and water.

These are the things that guide us, or maybe these are what I'm trying to find when I walk this river. But there's cow shit everywhere and the road keeps us away from the water.

See a woman sweeping strands of hay from her pavement; see a dog bark and follow us from window to window till we pass out of sight; see worn red barn doors now Guston-pink and peeling; see a slice of slate saying 'Bus Stop'; see a school with a brightly coloured wall and a black girl being met by a white woman; see fields of wheat ready to be cut; pass a Freemason's Hall, locked; hear the whirr of two bicycles, the cyclists looking at us in undisguised wonder; hear a chiffchaff; hear the dab dab dab of our sycamore sticks; hear my panting when we climb a hill; hear Craig ask, 'Some water?'; smell the animals in big, closed sheds; smell my sheughy sweat; smell crab apples, meadowsweet.

This is boring, says Craig...

There will be woods, there will be water. I'm limping on both legs. I could nun myself at the Cistercian Abbey.

The Bann is broad and warm here. Where Portglenone forest meets Glenone woods, water is wedded to tree and stone and a wildness that meets mildness. When we first entered the woods, we were haggard and harassed after hours of road dust and road roar. Then, a dropping away of the world, replaced with sudden smoothness of the sylvan: Sunfleck, silence and spongy woodchip paths leading down to the Bann.

Cherry, as always, first into the water. Down to skin and then in. A glide. A laugh at how quickly change comes. A pause as we are both pulled along. Then, a quiver of rain and the black surface of the Bann glistens.

We reach the sandy rim,

the vulva frock of the Bann.

We race into our togs.

A passing woman doesn't look.

A plump man walking

a black dog says, 'I don't swim.'

The plunge is surrender, the stroke

resistance, the balance buoyancy

carried in the river's horizontal.

Our legs kick the weight off as we flip

and furl, giddy with adjoining waterchrome.

Our feet suspend in bliss.

Skin and bones spread in easy capture

and the muscles pull them back

to the limb's line against the current.

Our arms are amber, legs green as jasper.

We breaststroke upstream, laughing towards One Oak Hill,

float downstream, otterine, svelted.

If she has a body, is a body, then this glossy slop

is the Bann's sex she carries everywhere.

You only have to move in her, to know.

      The road removes us.

      The river invites us back

      to time's deep body.

Portglenone to Bendooragh

Nurofen start, the bones crunchy with pain.

Headlines in the *Irish Times* say

cases of Covid are 'disimproving'.

A proper welcome in the Coffee Lab.

Eoin, the pharmacist, has read our interview

in the *Irish News*. Our O of surprise,

like the O of a hug. He wants the river seen,

secretly pays for our Americanos. The young barrista

donates bottled water and we feel almed.

We pass the bench where we ate

an Indian take-out, Craig's pack full of pilau rice,

his face free of vegan-range anxiety.

Each day, I get hungrier. I try to think of this as a symbol for something, but the belly beats the word, the meal walks ahead of the stanza. In Katesbridge, Banbridge, Portadown, Bannfoot, eating was a dutiful chore, but now, I feel gut bubbles and stomach strains. I want steaming rice and silky hummus and floury spuds and strong, strong coffee. I want Taytos and ale, Marmite on toast and Club Orange. I talk of recipes for baba ganoush and golden arancini. I walk for the sake of lunch, sweat for the sake of dinner.

It's the hottest July on record.
With fifteen minutes of rain in eight days,
can this be an Irish poem?

'Don't swim in the river or at the Barmouth
after rain. Rain washes in the effluent.'
It rose, it keeps rising, beyond the hushed

pandemic skies and dying seas.
Levels and percentages stay abstract,
like a high fever when you're well.

We pass signs to the golf club, the rugby club,
the Orange Lodge, the Masonic Hall and men's sheds.
Where are the women's places?

I count seventeen steps, feet dishevelled.
Every seventeen minutes during lockdown, the PSNI
were called out to post-romantic violence.

And the women, with an overnight bag,
still crossing the Irish Sea, to loosen and lose
the unwished for.

What happens, Craig asks, in an Orange Hall?

Orange men, black bowlers, orange flutes, white
                                   gloves, orange songs.

I barely know. They were places I refused to see.

I never knew anyone in an Orange Parade.

There's a lodge every few miles, windows meshed,
                                         fiercely bland.

Red Hands flutter but no people.

The powerful invisibles drive past, barely looking.

No Gaelic football posts mark the front gardens.

Dab-swing, dab-swing, dab-swing...

I got a job for twenty-five bob and I left,

left, left-right-left. I got a job for twenty-four bob

and I left, left, left-right-left...

My mind steps carefully in Ulster. Be careful what you think, be careful what you say. More than this, be careful about what you think you are allowed to say.

    Things like: Catholic areas seem more welcoming and less severe, both in buildings and in people. Insert something here about Presbyterian reserve, Protestant modesty. Sometimes, these stereotypes seem to hold water.

Now, let me be suspicious: You were always going to say that. You inherited this thought. It is mental undertow.

Now, let me be doubtful: There are no differences, and everywhere has been much the same. The architecture has been in square uniformity on both sides of the Bann, the houses separated from the landscape like curds from whey.

You have noticed only what you think the journey requires.

I am getting to know the North again.

People turned away from the river because it stank.

I turned away from the land because it hurt.

Funny that the Bann was mooted as the island's

dividing line, losing Belfast, keeping Derry.

What shape the battle might have taken.

There are still places of such anger

they need a peace wall. One hundred and sixteen places,

some attracting terror tourists.

The news reports that Soldier F

will not be prosecuted for killing two men

and another Bloody Sunday case folds.

How long can it go on? Prosecution.

How long can it not? Amnesty.

How long is long? Memory.

They say immigrants outnumber Unionists,

showing ways to be Irish with a hyphen.

Dab-swing, dab-swing, dab-swing...

In a book about landscape and folklore I've taken along, Wendell Berry writes: 'The test of imagination is, ultimately, not the territory of art or the territory of mind, but the territory underfoot.' Sometimes, when you read a phrase, you have to place a book down for a while.

Over a couple of days, these words rattle about in me like a stone in a tin can, or a heavy sleeper turning over on a rickety bed. Over field and stile and road and gate, and in unfamiliar rooms at night I weigh these words, knowing they mean something about what this journey is. But either I'm being a little stupid or I'm resisting.

Then I'm talking with Cherry on one of the numberless hedgerowed roads between Portglenone and Bendooragh. Not for the first time, we are reminding ourselves of why we are here and I hit on a word that makes sense of Berry: disappointment. I understand why the test is the territory underfoot.

Though we hail the imagination and celebrate its cosmic breadth, it is a narrow thing. Because why else would we journey, if imagining was enough? Why else suffer lumpy beds and shite coffee and the dreariness of Portadown if not to test the imagination against the granularity we find underfoot? So no, it is not just disappointment, it's what is left after disappointment. It is what is here.

We halt to read Li Bai, leaning on a railing.
'But slice water with a knife and water still flows.
Empty a wine cup to end grief and grief remains grief.'

We stravaigle off course for a standing stone
but find two derelict houses from the '20s and the '60s,
unblessed by ancient magic.

Neglected places used to frighten more than
sadden me forty years ago. A man in the country
in city clothes was a threat.

Dark spoored from him, from the land
he walked on, from beneath the land. A hiding place.
A weapon. A body. Jean McConville.

Turn swiftly, but not sharply,

as if you were blind, had seen nothing, no one.

That has passed. What is left?

New builds on shaved plots,

with no flourishes or frills,

that say 'keep out.'

So, who's my people? People with no people.

People with words picked with love as people.

But not people who say, 'We are all just people.'

The Bannside is rich in unimagined things: the grey grit slopped on the roadside every half mile; the concrete pipes that rib its banks; the way we are often distant from the river; the decaying stiles that offer both passage and hazard; the battalions of giant hogweed blooming and unfathomable; the slowness of hours but the quickness of the journey; the checked-shirted farmer's sons; bellies growing into their thirties; the guacamole like hair gel; the quietness of quoined houses. All these, and more, were unimagined but then seen.

And now nearing Coleraine, dots of memory congeal into pictures of her past:

'I went to a service in that church, there.'

'That's the field where I had wild sex.'

'The school bus took us this way. For years.'

'I was born in that hospital.'

But Cherry is a Lundy-queer who escaped to the rest of the world to be out of her corner of Ireland. Like so many on the island, she dreamed out, went out, then came out. In the '80s she left for London and swam in every current open to her: Queer Cinema, Troops Out, the buzz of a Boho London I'll never know.

She once took a car from one coast to another across a vast continent. She has lived in places beyond these islands and has spoken their languages. Often when I hear from her, she is in Scotland, Italy, Australia. She is a pebble thrown by a giant, skimming over Lough Neagh, always dreaming out. And of course, she cannot rest.

As we move towards the mouth, we are returning to a source. I feel it as much as the throb of my feet or the sweat down my back. Throughout our journey, Cherry has made mistakes. She's called the Lower Bann the Upper Bann, because she sees the end as a summit. And she keeps calling the mouth of the Bann the source, because she sees this journey as a return. I love her for these two mistakes, because they teach me what belonging is.

Craig sees red where I see orange,

sees food where I see weed,

sees chaffinch where I see bird,

sees hill where I see rath.

He teaches attention to smell,

to plumage and pelage,

to the feel of language in his mouth;

to the feel of white poplar leaves

between his fingers, to the underside

of living things; he's endlessly up for being here,

like a plant opening to the sun for more light,

more wisdom; he hums the dark

hedges inside himself.

He sees what I block out,

the signatures of bigots,

the wounds' crust fear fosters,

now speaking in a third voice

like the offspring of divorce.

We listen like a bell to a clapper,

read the rings in an old oak.

We're characters from an Irish Tarot:

the Green Man and the Orange Woman.

Cherry listens as I call out plants from the roadside, birds from the air, trees from the wood. Along the way, she accepts my offerings of sorrel, yarrow, wild marjoram, black mustard, Jack-by-the-Hedge. Whether bitter or tart, the new is always sweet to Cherry. There is no baulking, no cringing, in anything she does. I make note: this is a lesson I must learn.

As we walk, names leap to my tongue, the green world

throbs with names for this keen man to catch.

'Yellowhammer in the hawthorn!'

'Hemlock by the road there.'

'Dryad's Saddle on that stump of oak.'

It seems nature is second nature. But it only seems. I couldn't always tell oak from sycamore or wren from dunnock. In Thornhill, the council estate I was raised on, fewer names were needed, fewer even known. Plants were just plants. Birds, just birds. I was young, eight maybe, and asked Mum the name of a tree in our front garden. The door ajar, she turned to me, eyes weary.

'It's a tree.'

Too-keen as always, I pursued. 'But what *kind* of tree?'

'It's just a *fucking tree!*' and Mum disappeared into the darkness of the house.

And for a while, I kept schtum. For a while, plants were just plants, birds, just birds, land just land. This truth became second nature. But later, name-hunger made me ask and keep asking. I realised a name was a key to seeing. Names made the green world throb. Names made it tart, bitter, sweet.

These two things then bend our lives into their shapes: questions that are askable, and what we say in answer.

I don't want to say, I don't have to say.

It would be simpler not to say and fit that old adage

'Whatever you say, say nothing' that versed my girlhood.

Today I mention a father being thrown through a window

by a brother, the night patrol to find his plastered body,

the day patrol to lock the drinks cupboard, to sweep

dirt and hoover glass, to serve salted cashews
with the G&Ts. Like stepping into a ruin, there's safety
in it because the roof has already fallen in. He broke
blood's rule of touch. Several walls are barely standing.
The unimagined things imagined. Unimaginable.
The walls are girls. The door is always open to him.
If the crime is hidden, so is what delivers us.
Craig listens, keeps listening among the moss.

> In plain sight signs hide
> Orangemen, gunmen, Jesus.
> How's the form, boyo?

Bendooragh to Barmouth

Only singing can move us along the long Vow Road,

the Bann Valley Scenic Route, where the river stays schtum.

No tales from the tombstones of the families

driven out in 1772 for being wild Presbyterians.

Vows can't shorten the tongue of the long Vow Road,

or quieten its deep guarded consonants.

There are names I know at Kildollagh:

McCulloch, Clark, Hughes in a row, on a raised bed,

once friends at a dinner table, full, flirting and fired up.

My parents want to be ash. I will mourn them, arms open

to the unfixed mineral of the sea.

By bank and on road, I've met more people in the last eight
days than in the last eighteen months. The fact frightens me.
Each person offers a sliver of life, part of a whole I'll never
know. It makes me - almost - crave for those eighteen months
again, crave to be back on my arse in my small flat, standing
up in my small flat, sweating and shivering and stalling in
my small fucking flat. Because now, even for this keen man,

the slivers of strangers' lives are exhausting. Fitness of lung and foot are still there, but another kind of fitness has been lost. And as this walk closes, I wonder if I have tramped only the surface.

The map sprouts Moraig. Wee Doc. Kelly's. Spuds.

Drunk sheets, whisper boys; failure at water skis

and boys who water-skied; chasing milk delivery boys

who glided on something else. I couldn't wait to be bad.

Here, at the clake of the Loughan, dredgers in the '30s

unearthed a bronze saucer, banked by the river's vault,

with three birds' heads in the same spiral

that signals the underworld at Newgrange.

This treasured triskele, from when art was spirit,

bridges Bann to Boyne, to the Mesolithic skeins

of settlements, signs and sense, shaping

distance by the same full moon.

The map and the land are awkward lovers, they relate only by forgiving the clumsy hands which try to translate one space into another. And with this land, I am the awkwardest lover, my hands the clumsiest hands. I am the son of the map, the grandson of the wide view, the great-grandson of sentimental song:

On the banks of the Bann it was there I first met her,
She appeared like some goddess or Egypt's fair queen,
Her eyes were like diamonds or the stars brightly shining.
She's the fairest of all in this wide world I've seen.

Here the Bann is a swift / broad sleeve / through woodland/

a cruiser-bruiser-pleasure / where sunlight picks out

moss on larch /

fast-food cartons on the picnic table/

gay cruising cars parked/ windows rolled down/

'Grand day' above a small dock/ a curve in water/

shaded by trees/

holding a hard cheek of desire/ looking for like/

shaded at Camus/ the look that knows itself/ a twinkle

enfolded in shame/ four geese overhead/ always keeping

a look-out/ the birds that fly with one eye open/

there's a word for that/ a kiss with one eye open/

pilgrims came to kneel/ at the Bullaun Stone/ to touch

the dent of healing water/ that never dries.

A cookie-cutter coffee shop in London, 2017. A place where it's easy to forget there's a river. It's over a year since the vote and the Great British media have begun to realise there's an island over there, a border over there. And it's bloody complicated, too bloody complicated. Our coffees are sipped as we moan, nod, wince, remoan. News crews are out and asking people to draw the Irish border. Some complain they were never taught this stuff as they scrawl a line from Galway to Dublin. It's just too bloody complicated. Others say the Irish are just being difficult, should just lump it, that they lost, we won. I shake my head as we get up to leave.

'It's a funny time to be English.'

She stops. 'You consider yourself English?' she says.

'Yes,' I say. 'What else would I be?'

'Oh,' she says, and pauses, looks a little skyward.

Like migrating eel or salmon, at the Cutts, we move

from fresh to saltwater, become catadromous.

I sigh to reach Mountsandel, a plenty ancestors could not

forsake, and stayed: Ireland's first. Above Creeve's Falls,

they settled in the hazel wood. Hock of deer, bone of boar,
chinked flint, buried in a hilltop scatter. Few human bones

mark out this birthplace of Mesolithic roots that later
drew the giant navel of a Norman keep.

We circle a huge grassy crown worn by the tentacles
of Bannview, Bannside, Bannfield, Bann Court

Coleraine sells. A roundabout announces 'NI100',
a low-key birthday card. Will it see another century?

Of all the conversations we have by the river, those of family
feature most. It's a story of annoyance, of unalignment, of
awkwardness and of love. We could not have this annoyance
without this love. We are the black sheep, we say. We are the
ones who went away, we say. These stories outpace our stride,
their length outstretches this road from source to mouth.

Home is where the map runs into blue.
I'm always returning to blue, misnaming mouth
as source. We end where I began.
And as the river cycles to cloud to bog,
I cycle from land to air, to sea, to city,

collecting words fresh to me and lost to me.

I become different people, pronounce peace

differently, think about difference

differently, learn the easy persistence of flow,

the malleability of water, the point of margins.

The river is not what I came looking for.

What the journey gives is walking in sync

with another, going foot for leg to learn what

can't be found in books – an eight-day echo

filling displacement with a trusting place.

Weeks before we left, Cherry asked that if sometimes on the walk, we could just be silent. I understand. I can be an unremitting torrent of syllables and sometimes, I know, people wish they could slide away. So, I agree. There will be times without talk, when we simply scan our senses and suck in silence.

This doesn't happen. We never stop speaking, and even if I try, there is a comment about people, place and past, always on her lips. When we are not tired, talk is easy. When we are tired, talk pushes us forward. Is this because talking and noticing are the same thing?

We grit the road with words, make a formless path in vowels and consonants. So the talking never stops, because when else do we have the chance to talk about these things?

We make a drystone wall of talk, weighing the right

stone, fitting the right angle to hold time back,

coax lichen, share a love of moss. We paughle along.

We laugh at being paughles – lumps of humans,

creating a new etymology of friendship.

I will die now, the power of circular completion being

so strong. New line, old circle. Irish named it *soathar:*

the hole fish make in a sandy riverbed to spawn.

> River turns sandy,
>
> turns salty, returns
>
> to the Atlantic.

This pilgrimage has forced me to walk the frail line of my desire. The English child who was never quite English enough, is a man who will never be Irish enough. Those times of not trying enough, or of trying too hard. People here have been puzzled when I've shown knowledge of place and politics, shown familiarity with the histories and stories that have built this place. They've asked me, 'why do you care?', because English people don't care.

Why do I care? Only because of a bruised palette of school maps, borrowed books, a grandfather's tales, a mother's last journey, the tilt of a jig, the weave of a knot. Even more than background and the ground underfoot as we've walked this Bann.

At the journey's start, Peter handed me
a balled pair of thick, green-grey socks
of moss, feather and lichen, knitted by
spiderwebs. As my finger entered, the soft,
warm nest said gossamer.
I can still hear it in my hands.
Can the fabric of home feel like that?
Light and airy to hold, remarkably holding.

My father would call me to watch the sunset
at the Barmouth he can no longer see,
no longer walk to; Mussenden, our borrowed
Tivoli, a circular dream of books, lit up by
April's dusk: an echo with no shape attached.

My nonagenarian pop, my world journeyman,
is at the head of the road, full of holes.
He grasps sand from sentences in waves
that break but are no longer part of the same shore.
'Has my wife perished?' he asks of sundown.
He can't tell if he's missed his own bereavement.
'No, Dad, she's in the next room.'

I am forever raising the dead or laying
them to rest again in the freshly furrowed
soil. I command his underworld with
corrections so meek he won't notice the shame
of his mistakes; erasing and rebuilding
his kin in rags, as if life and death were as fluid
and intertwined as we believe in our moments
of greatest transcendence. How many
unspoken chasms he must visit, dangled
in a near century of lives, loves and losses, some
more pressing than the 'we' we can offer him
in the sieved present. 'You *are* home, Dads.
This is your house, paid for with good money.'

I need somebody to love me,
need somebody to carry me home to
San Francisco and bury my body there.

Can the river belong to me now? Are the bonny banks of the
Bann now my banks? Is Banbridge my bridge? I wanted this
pilgrimage to have the thrill of a sky-wide beginning with the
comfort of a closed end. This was the story I'd tell. But it's the
other way around. The start was a trickle in a marshy field, and
the end is the Atlantic.

I belong to these questions, like a son belongs to a mother.

Our blood joints walk the final mile at Portstewart.

Family converges on the long bow of the strand.

Beyond the Valley of the Stones, the waves' roar trails

in the marram grass. Roots of an extinct wood split the path.

Towards Limavady, turbine siblings, do the same thing

at different speeds, with differing aptitude. Two refuse

to budge their triskelion blades.

On the golf course: innocuous flags.

Trees arch with wind at Ballywoolen. My brother Gavin

is saying something about large clams, called geegans,

and the sea bass once coming in to feed on them.

Blood is a river we step into twice, home in our veins,

elsewhere in our arteries, fed by the same breath.

A rescue helicopter thrums overhead. Oystercatchers

question the machair. Black-headed gulls marshal

a fallen pier. We cross the arc of Duggan's Bay.

There's a deep privacy on this side of the dunes.

On winter's runway for whooper swans,

a hide, where yeasty clabber dissolves. The tide

pulls light seaward: the river belongs to the terns.

What else has the river carried from Slieve Muck
as well as our watching? A bird's thran peeping,
driftwood, detergent bottles. I have carried love,
clarified with breath's polish, for the itinerary of flux.

If you were in your bed lying and thinking on dying
One sight of the bonny Bann banks, your sorrow you'd give o'er
Or if you were one hour, down in yon shady bower
Pleasure would surround you, you'd think on death no more.

A river always drowns too soon, the maw
unstoppable. They once believed a woman,
like Tuag or Bó Ann, could gently temper
Manannán, their sweetness yielded to
edgelessness – the island's shared fear.
The death of the Bann foretold their own,
a home that exists without bounds.

Desire spills for the catalyst.
I am more salmon than dolmen.
I hold absence so close I can't feel it.
The river will leave with me, living from its
own source that I visit – always visiting –

The lighthouse becomes the walk's end
with no discussion. Will the pilgrimage end
at the house, at Aldergrove, when my banjaxed
feet heal or in these lines?

We touch the base of the lighthouse, hug and toss
our sticks into the river-sea where the salmon
and the eels come and leave –
less come, less leave.

More than once I was ready to follow
the river fully with the ease of never swimming back,
to lose my body to a more buoyant form.
I can't yet submit to swell, to slouster in depth,
but try to breathe it into my confined joy.

Those days outside, un-windowed, door-less,
soft-cornered, thinning to road, to river, housed
by sky, bred a hobo love. Pain tramped through us
to a billowing beyond matter, the river's lesson.
At matter's sore edge, none of it mattered.

We walk back along the pier. We are sixty percent water.
Today we are sixty percent Bann. The water has friends.

This can be an Irish poem

Postscript

Months later, her brother is driving her from Belfast airport down to Portstewart. She knows the road – the M2, the slip road off to Ballymoney and Coleraine, the new by-pass at the Frosses, the sweep of roundabouts. As they drive, the afternoon sun is setting and the winter trees have lost more of their leaves than in London. Shadows sharpen and lengthen in a northern light that can make October more stunning than July, when a warmth in the wind is a bonus and the white clouds are dramatically high. Her accent changes to meet his, all part of the incremental adjustments homecoming enacts in the body. Her gestures begin to mirror his. She senses another mirroring happening to the east of the road where the Bann runs. She can't see it, but she knows it's there and she now knows where she could go to meet it along the route: below the crossroad of churches at Portglenone; next to the woodland path at Castleroe; beside the posts of a fallen pier at Duggan's Bay. This knowing places her more deeply in the lie of the land as if someone is breathing in tandem with her. It's a new intimacy with home that she didn't know she was seeking or why. Learning it as if it wasn't hers has somehow made it belong to her more, the forty years of living away, near the Thames, the Seine, the Hudson, all one river, heading towards the one ocean. As the car reaches seventy, she slows everything down and is walking, looking, remembering the feeling of measuring the journey home in footsteps and the roving energy and excitement of the conversation that never stopped And even though the walk was arduous at times, dull at others, there was a kind of resting in it that was new to her. Despite the years of homophobia and sectarianism, the landscape didn't question her presence. The car's headlights light up the drive down towards the house and she can hear the waves. She leaps from the car to hug the salt and seaweed smell of the wind.

This will be the last time she will see her father alive. He will die five months after the pilgrimage ends. She will sit at the dining table while the others are in the kitchen and hold his hands. They are square, delicate hands with tender pale palms: indoor hands. Hands that could fold a shirt so that it looked new. A draper's hands that could pass under a spread bolt of cloth to help its colours and textures catch all kinds of light. These are the hands that taught her to swim, levelled under her belly, cupping her chin, ready to haul her up when she went under. Her dad had been an all-weather swimmer, plunging into the Atlantic and coming up, startled pink and gasping with vigorous joy. No wetsuit, no concept of wild swimming.

There will be candles lit in the dining room and he will lean over and try to blow them out to save money – his habitual frugality outwitting his terminal confusion. She will talk quietly to him. He recognises her voice more than her face. Once, he slipped a generation or two and asked her if she was a Breen. She swam in the stream of ancestors. 'Closer to you than that,' she said. 'Is that a fact?' he said. But she is a Breen, a McVitty, a Smyth. He will hold her hands and look into her face and she knows this is the intimacy she will lose.

Many of the names will go when he goes. Their chant resounds through her. Her poems tally names, like totting up at the end of a long Saturday in the shop, passing over a pile of cash bound in a rubber band, with the total written in small figures on the top note.

*

Months later in the little flat in Brighton, the showerhead is over him, hot water draining the cold from his body. He raises an arm amid the steam and catches sight of the shamrock on his un-sunned skin. Sometimes, most of the time, he doesn't see it. Like a neighbour's house, the local woods or a natal river, some things become familiar enough to be hidden. Our bodies too are places, after all. He knew beforehand that part of the journey happens before the actual trip. It happens in our imaginations, in the thrills and uncertainties we press into the future before we take to the river, the mountain, the road. But he knows too that even after a journey is done, it is not finished.

He looks at his arm again and notes now, how after a quarter of a century on his skin, the tattoo has begun to blear. The emerald green is less than verdant, the outline diffused. Below his shamrock the word 'Ireland', once in a neat little scroll, is fuzzy. Its calligraphy is melting into a scrawl. He twists his wrist, shuts the shower off. But he's a writer now, and writers don't let things like this just flow past them.

He pulls back the shower curtain and steps out, remembering the help he gave his mother on her final visit to Banbridge. Often, he finds himself there. What has welled here? What does this noticing of his arm, remembrance of his mother, mean? Soon he is dry and whilst dressing, the autumn coolness takes its turn to steal back the heat the water had given only minutes before.

And all of a sudden yes, he thinks, yes: it is restlessness. He pauses, dressed now, warming back up in his ever-scruffy clothes. What wells now, is how this restlessness between one island and another will never stop for him, cannot stop, should not stop. It is a restlessness that drives forward and bows round and becomes a torrent, then a trickle. He realises he needs it to be this way. And it is not despite the blear and scrawl and diffusion, it is because of it.

He fondles his phone as he tramps down the thinly carpeted stairs. He thinks about calling her, thinks about telling her all of this. He knows she will understand. Him. The journey. He wants to let her know that being footsore and dust-stained was easy. Passing out of the mountains and towards the ocean was easy. But building little dams and seeing what wells there, this will always be difficult.

But he waits, because he will see her soon, won't he? He just does not want to seem too keen.

*

It may seem weird, but she picks out one of her father's checked shirts. It's white with green and brown checks. It is slightly frayed at the collar which will suit him better. It may be a little too small, but he wears his shirts open over a worn, faded T-shirt. She won't say it is her father's until he tries it, accepts it. Then she will say. And she will feel her eyes pricking because he likes it and it becomes him and this is how family is made.

Since her father's death, Ireland itself has moved into the hole in her cosmos, like a parent. Death is closer, everyone knows that, but what she didn't know was how Ireland would shift, towards and around, in a fathering hug – but 'hug' is too sweet – it's more of an enclosing, a setting like a stone held in a ring. It can be sharp as well as soft. It's asking something of her. As he lay in the Causeway Room of the funeral home, with a pallor he never knew when alive, that made his dark eyebrows youthful and pronounced, she asked her Da's body, 'Should I come back?' We think of ancestors as ancient and long gone, but here he was, crossed over into that name overnight. And she became aware of the questions the river asked, how its knowledge of transition could become hers, in the face of loss and her life's most massive change. The sea below the house, she thinks, is always there with its showy vastness, while the river, beyond the Valley of the Stones and the rocky pier, waits to be sought out. Its quieter language drew her and she had to become quiet to hear it.

Ulsterisms

banjaxed	wrecked
the carry of the sky	the drift of clouds
clabber	mud
clake	bend in a river
go foot for leg	go fast
gunk	disappointment
haugh	uncultivated land
	near a river
holding a hard cheek	keeping a secret
jaup	lap of water against a boat
jibble	dribble, spill
juking	crouching down out of sight

the moon is on her back	sign of rain because the crescent moon on her back collects water within her horns
paughle	a lump of dirt or manure; to walk with difficulty
nothing but black water	anticipate total failure
sheugh(y)	a ditch
slouster	dabble in water; work in wet conditions
stravaigle	to wander; from Medieval Latin extravagari, to wander beyond the limits
streel	wander aimlessly; streeler – a loose woman
strone	stream of milk from a cow's teat, a pour of tea
thran	stubborn
wheen	large amount

Acknowledgements

Many thanks are due to the Tyrone Guthrie Centre at Annaghmakerrig where the seeds of this collaboration were sown. Thanks also to Paul Maddern and the Mill Retreat where the writing began. Thank you also to those who made the journey possible: the Northern Ireland Arts Council, the University of Greenwich and the University of Brighton. We are indebted to people we met along the watter's (sic Ulster-Scots) way: Elizabeth Magowan, Peter Wilson, Frankie Conlon, and Steve Craig. And to the lovely Margaret who invited us in for watter and books. Thanks also to Kerrie Curzon, Kate Carroll, Sal Sinclair, Elaine Gaston, Emer Lyons, Ailna Smyth, Gavin, Julie and Campbell Smyth, Autozone Cars, Siobhan Snowden, Peter Brown, Andrea Johnson, Ed Bennett, Xenia Pestova, Francois Vincent, Eimear McGeown and Aoife Ní Bhriain. Our huge thanks also go to Sean Campbell for not holding back with his encouragement and belief in the book and its hybrid nature.